About the Author

I am a writer, poet and mother of one based in Chelmsford Essex. I grew up in North London Enfield and have always had a passion for reading, storytelling and creative expression. My son has been my biggest fan and motivation for my stories.

Afro Boy and the Bears

Phoebe Raphael

Afro Boy and the Bears

Olympia Publishers
London

www.olympiapublishers.com
OLYMPIA PAPERBACK EDITION

A CIP catalogue record for this title is available from the British Library.

ISBN: 978-1-78830-805-2
First Published in 2021

Olympia Publishers
Tallis House
2 Tallis Street
London
EC4Y 0AB

Printed in Great Britain

Dedication

This book is dedicated to Elijah–Dumas, who always has time for an adventure
and who had the most amazing Afro in the world.

Afro boy is a young lad who is tall lanky and fair,
who has really long legs and gigantic red hair.

He lives in a cottage with his mother and father too,
on a hill named Topsy Mews.

One hot afternoon his mother yelled out,
"My dearest son, won't you please help me out?".

So off he went with a whiz and zoom,
past the butcher shop and Copper Mill school.

Afro boy took a short cut, through Bush Hill Park Wood.
He cycled and pedaled as fast as he could.

Soon he got tired and thirsty too,
so he sat under a tree in the late afternoon.

Afro boy spotted a cottage not far ahead.
He knocked on the door and popped round his head.

"Is anyone home?" he yelled before walking inside.
But nobody answered and no one replied.

The smell of warm toast soon tickled his nose,
so he followed the scent as he walked on tip toes.

Then in came a bear as big as can be,
wearing an apron and glasses to see.

In came another, he was a small little cub.
He stared at Afro boy whilst sucking his thumb.

"We are baking bread, you can help us bake too,"
said Daddy Bear as he led the way through.

Together they mixed, kneaded and baked,
they had loaves upon loaves of freshly baked breads and cakes.

It was getting late and the sun started to set.
"You must head off home," Mummy Bear said with a fret.

Mummy, Daddy and Baby Bear waved him good bye.
"Please come again soon," Mummy Bear said with a sigh.

So off he pedaled with a whiz and a zoom,
back through Bush Hill Park Wood, and past Copper Mill school...

Past the butchers and safely on Topsy Mews,
at last he was home to deliver the news.

"Mum guess what, I've got all your bread,"
Afro boy shouted as he pranced and leapt.

"I helped to make it with the three bears," he explained.
"Three bears?" his mother repeated, "how very strange."

But the bread looked amazing and tasted a treat.
"We must thank the three bears," Afro boy's father agreed.

So they posted a basket filled with delights,
to thank the three bears for being so nice.